The Secret Fawn

words by
Kallie George

pictures by
Elly MacKay

tundra

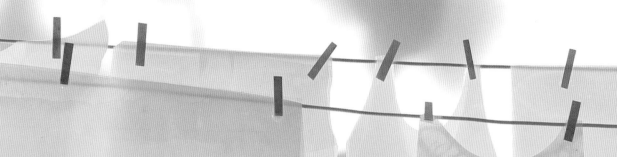

Text copyright © 2021 by Kallie George
Illustrations copyright © 2021 by Elly MacKay

Tundra Books, an imprint of Penguin Random House Canada Young Readers,
a division of Penguin Random House of Canada Limited

All rights reserved. The use of any part of this publication reproduced, transmitted in any form or by any
means, electronic, mechanical, photocopying, recording, or otherwise, or stored in a retrieval system,
without the prior written consent of the publisher — or, in case of photocopying or other reprographic
copying, a license from the Canadian Copyright Licensing Agency — is an infringement of the copyright law.

Library and Archives Canada Cataloguing in Publication
Title: The secret fawn / Kallie George ; Elly Mackay.
Names: George, K. (Kallie), 1983- author. | MacKay, Elly, illustrator.
Identifiers: Canadiana (print) 20190223685 | Canadiana (ebook) 20190223758 | ISBN 9780735265165
(hardcover) | ISBN 9780735265172 (EPUB)
Subjects: LCGFT: Picture books.
Classification: LCC PS8563.E6257 S43 2021 | DDC jC813/.6—dc23

Published simultaneously in the United States by Tundra Books of Northern New York,
an imprint of Penguin Random House Canada Young Readers,
a division of Penguin Random House of Canada Limited

Library of Congress Control Number: 2019954620

Edited by Tara Walker and Elizabeth Kribs
Designed by Kelly Hill
The illustrations in this book were created using ink, paper and light.
The text was set in Bembo.

Printed and bound in China

www.penguinrandomhouse.ca

1   2   3   4   5   25   24   23   22   21

Penguin
Random House
tundra   TUNDRA BOOKS

For Elly

K.G.

To Lily and Koen.
Thank you for the
dandelions.

E.M.

This morning,
Mama saw a deer.
Dad and Sara saw it too.

But I didn't.
I was getting dressed
all by myself.

I always miss everything.

I missed the shooting stars
because I go to bed too early.

I missed picking the first apple
because I am too short.

And now
I missed the deer.

While Mama
makes pancakes,
I slip outside,
with a sugar cube
in my pocket.

The sun is soft and gold.
The grass is wet and tickles my toes.

There is no sign of the deer.

Whish . . . I hear something.
Is that the deer behind the apple trees?

No, it's just some leaves,
dancing down.

Flick! I see a flash of brown.
Is that the deer?

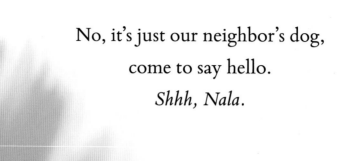

No, it's just our neighbor's dog,
come to say hello.
Shhh, Nala.

Splash! Something's by the pond.
Is that the deer, taking a drink?

No, it's just a bird, searching like me.

Crick–crack . . .

Is that the deer, rustling some branches?

No, it's just a squirrel,
nibbling its breakfast.

My stomach rumbles for *my* breakfast.

I sigh and sit down.
I don't care if it's wet.
Carefully, I place the sugar cube on a rock.

Maybe the deer is hungry too.
Maybe it will come back.

I listen . . . nothing.
And then, I look . . .

I see something!

In the bushes. Not a deer . . .

A fawn. A baby deer.
Golden and soft like the sunlight.
Quiet as a whisper.
Little like me.

It looks up at me and blinks.

"Hello," we say with our eyes.

I watch, until it rises, wobbly,
and heads into the woods,
to find its mama.

I rise and head home
to find my mama too.

Mama is waiting for me
with a plate of pancakes.

"Did you see the deer?"
she asks.

I shake my head.
Because I didn't.

I saw its fawn.